The Unspoken Words—For What Remains Unsaid

By

Yasmeen Jawhar

E-Book ISBN: 978-1-969066-57-3

Paperback ISBN: 978-1-969066-58-0

Hardcover ISBN: 978-1-969066-59-7

Published by: Columbus Book Publishers

www.columbusbookpublishers.com/

Printed in the United States of America

Dedication

To the ones we lost too soon, to illness, to silence, struggling in the darkness to the fading shadows of memory.

Though time, illness, and sorrow stole your days, they could not steal your essence. You live in the depths of my words, in the pulse of my spirit, our culture that continues, in the love that lingers eternal and unyielding.

This book is for you, my vow that you are always here with us, and never forgotten.

Zein Al Zoubi

Monzer Jawhar

Jude Jawhar

Mohammed Mahmoud Jawhar/Ishtar Lazuli

Mohammed El-Araj

Asaad Alattereh

Fatima Khalid Shaker

Fathallah Abdulatif Jowhar

May you be in God's mercy. In a place of solace, peace, and contentment.

Table of Contents

Page Left Blank Intentionally

1

The Darkness

The night is dark, but the day feels darker,

without you near.

It feels harder now, when you

have to feel and reach out,

with no light and barely any help.

I move, blinded, despite everything.

And when the beating heart stops,

there will be no path other than,

a quiet drift into the darkness,

with memories to pass.

And the only consolation is

knowing you are ok.

And in this desperation,

I hold one truth close that someday,

I know I will see you again.

2

The Quiet

And in the quiet, in the shadows,

when all is still, and free of distraction.

That's when the thoughts creep up.

Honestly, they never left;

They were always there, just quieter.

but now, amplified by the darkness,

they remind me, of pain and sadness.

With glimpses of memories, windows into

what happened, or pictures of

what could have been, lie still.

And nothing can make them disappear,

or help you see clearly what your path is;

and where your destiny lies.

3

The Thoughts

"You're crazy.

How could you think that way?"

someone will say; to which you have

no answer, in disbelief.

But for you, it's a beg, it's a prayer:

Please believe me.

I swear it's not nothing.

Inside, it will be.

Not a made-up story.

My thoughts; all consuming.

I try to shake them,

but like quicksand,

they suck you down again.

Like an hourglass,

stuck being flipped back –

to start over again.

Can't you understand?

It's not a choice.

It's a rock and a hard place,

A wall and a bridge,

a finish line way out in the

distance trying to run to it,

to cross.

I don't even care what

number I am when I complete it.

I just want to go home.

4

The Near, The Far

In the in-between,

in the parts, all the ways;

in the dark.

Whether close, or far from here,

we seek to find a beating heart,

a love that's clear.

Ours, a far away thought,

a feeling... no, a whisper.

Time and again,we've caught

these inner contemplations,

with winding complications,

only to be addressed;

to be claimed, to be confessed.

We drown our sadness,

our cares, to bear witness

to the weight of our own dares.

Dare I bare my own sacred ideas,

my beliefs, my considerations

that help me confront my wars?

And near or far,

in the stillness of night,

I'll question, I'll fight

these selfless, defenseless

pains and this endless plight.

5

The Mirror

The glass; where the edges touch,

where your breath lingers on.

I see an image of myself:

not quite me, not quite true.

Can you keep the crown?

Tilt your head to feel its weight

a heaviness; no one can lift

but you.

Only the burden

felt upon your shoulders.

You can't remove it.

You sigh while you adjust it.

How can I leave this?

Shaken by my core,

Where would I go?

My resemblance, a persona

made up by many.

A betrayal.

A portrayal I store,

trying to be something,

trying to be alright.

That reflection...

is it well enough?

You must raise it, and never give in,

but always fight.

6

The Reflection

Words are read

through the windows of my soul.

I hold on so tight,

I don't ever want to let go.

I took my time,

day and night,

to wonder, realize,

and perfect my own light.

It gave me pain.

It gave me strength.

It gave me inner sight.

Staring into the night sky,

breathing in the warm air.

torn into pieces,

wondering how I got this far.

Dear God...

am I alone?

Please, sing the music

that gives me wings,

So that I may see

my true self,

my reflection.

7

The Yesterday

A faded memory

of yesterdays;

my mind's own play.

(what's done is done.)

Deceiving and perceiving

its own rotten core,

like the apple

hiding a worm,

our own discomfort,

a heart's sore.

In agony and affliction,

a struggled depiction.

If only, I could do it all again,

I'd say: take it back,

tortured,

to redo, to rerun.

But in fact,

I cannot;.
It's terminated,
ached, and drenched
in despair, in denial.

What's at an end:
a sick torment, so vile.

Powerless, helpless
to bring back what's been.

All you can do
is strive to look forward.

No sense in looking back
To what's over and over.

11 稲口

8

The Tomorrow

What you seek,

you will find

a closed box

of a mind.

Once opened,

true despair unfolds,

because once opened,

you've released

a desperation:

dangerous risks

and invitations

to bid a foreword farewell

to what once was.

A goodbye, a pain?

Mourning to a pause,

unguided affliction.

Because you must look again,

Seek to fly.

Don't look back, struggle forward to find the pieces, a peace for your
mind.

For troubled,

you will always be,

unless you

consider an eventuality

of finality.

9

The Fate

Some days,

It's heavy.

The days are so long,

and some days run through each other,

and it's hard to remember

what happened.

You try to humble yourself

and try to see the good

around you,

but the heaviness just drowns out

the sounds.

And all you see and breathe in

is heartfelt, deep sorrow

no one needs to see,

and no one needs to feel

what you have.

Just smile, and it'll all be okay.

This life is a born loneliness;

it divides man and people.

It takes you and scrapes

every last drop of genuineness.

The loneliness and hunger

drive you to extinction.

It deprives man of generosity.

And the rich take,

and the young dream.

In it all, we stand and watch as it passes

with every minute,

every hour,

 and the seasons' changes,

and we change.

We have, we take.

We keep, we hate.

And all that was once good and great

leaves us like the leaves,

Drop from heaviness and fate.

10

The Distance

And when my bones are too old,

I pray you seek me out,

To find me wherever you are,

to live out the rest of our years

with me, together:

to laugh and cry, to reminisce,

to hold, to kiss.

And while grey and wrinkled,

we still look in the mirror,

see the young and vivacious

energy full, hearts a twinkle

enough to sit in peace,

holding hands,

quiet in existence to be with me,

no matter the distance.

11

The Desired

There are not enough words

no words,

that can ever be said

to gain my acceptance

of whatever happened.

The winds have died down,

the flowers all dead

lost all patience from

waiting and wanting.

In every breathe,

stopped every minute,

the pages dried

where my pen

stopped writing,

but the story

couldn't be told.

Stolen from time in the Fall

when all the leaves blew away

we couldn't have stayed,

so tired

from being Starved

from that which is so desired.

12

The Simultaneous

It wasn't your eyes,

it wasn't your smile

it was your heart,

just like mine,

beating, dreaming

of a place

with happiness,

with warmth.

Oh, those dreams;

if only a reality

could exist

for you and me.

Because it was your eyes

and your smile

In them shaped us

But life said otherwise

And our paths might not cross

And it may take a while.

13

The Heaven

They get to be free

to fly away.

Where do all souls go?

Why do I cry?

A reason for rain?

A type of pain.

It's a good thing,

but maybe if I die,

I can be amongst them,

where all souls go,

where the sun hides,

and no one knows.

The wind blows,

My face touching

the air, condemns

this pure mayhem.

Do you understand

how this flows?

That this bigger thing in the sky

Is immensely greater than you and I?

14

The Beautiful Good Thing

A Poem about Grief and Loss

In memory of Zein, my lovely Niece

Dear Zein....

Those big brown beautiful eyes,

that smile that shines

and brightens up a room so full.

your personality, so great

it was never overseen.

Dear Zein....

We all miss you,

we all cry and speak of you in everything

Every second, every moment,

every memory, you are in our minds,

in the raindrops and in the butterflies,

and the birds when they sing.

Dear Zein....

We are scared to lose you,

we already did.

But scared our human brains will forget,

we scrape up and grab tightly,

As if every we might lose our grip.

Dear Zein....

I hope you knew

we all loved you.

We all enjoyed your time,

we admired your grace and beauty,

and your mind.

your zeal and determination,

that excitement you had for life.

We laugh sometimes thinking of our

conversations.

Dear Zein....

It's so crazy how much

a person can affect us.

It's so hard to breathe sometimes;

the weight of it all

ties us down.

Mentally, we're all trying to survive,

stand up, and not fall.

we don't want to let you know of our sadness.

Dear Zein...

We love you so much-

loved you.

We are desperate;

we want one more of everything:

a hug, a kiss,

a moment, a picture,

a laugh, a time.

Life is so hard just remembering

instead of living it with you.

Dear Zein...

We hope and pray

you are at peace.

You always gave—

so admirable and virtuous

from your heart to all things,

generous to all creatures,

animals and people.

Dear Zein...
Gentle and sweet girl,

we lost so much

when we lost you

a missing puzzle piece,

a part of our hearts

that will never leave,

waiting to meet.

Dear Zein...
There will always be goodbyes in life,

but the goodbye to you,

the leaving you,

the leaving us too soon,

is and will be one of the

hardest goodbyes in our lives.

Dear Zein...
We can't express it in any other way

the grief, it comes in waves:

constant tears, upset, fears,

anger, and regrets.

it's like a horrible dream

we keep thinking its fake,

that maybe we'll wake.

But broken hearts don't mend,

especially with this end.

Dear Zein...

you were and are

magnificent.

Love you always and forever.

There will never be enough paper,

or ink, or feathers,

until we see each other again.

Rest easy, my dear.

Hugs and kisses

we cannot wait!

15

The Waves

And by the shores

the farness, darkness,

and unbreathable waves

kept me from getting to you.

Never again to hear your

Voice over the crashes

and cries.

Weathering a storm,

not only in reality,

but in my heart.

That death – my sweet

reprise came for me too,

soon.

So that this time sitting,

waiting, would pass,

and we would be together

once again.

16

The Death

Forgetfulness and forgiveness

is a gift,

and it's wrapped up

in only some minds.

Whereas others find

complicity, complacency,

and are chained to a

hard remembrance

and maliciousness.

They're tied down

by their thoughts in a

vindictive manner,

and are actually only freed

when the Angel of Death

comes knocking

at their door.

Just then,

their realization

is of their own hearts

at fault.

17

The Flame

There, sometimes there

a glimpse, a hint,

a tiny flame.

It wishes to burn,

to consume

everything

the very thing untamed.

This world,

the oxygen, the air;

it breathes it in

with such desire

and gusto.

It yearns,

striking the coals

of this Earth.

And with wood,

it envelopes the land

one by one,

flame by flame

engulfing life

with the lights

of red, yellow, and orange.

Setting over us,

as the sunset does

larger and more powerful

it grows.

Its heat and warmth

overtaking

so satisfying,

yet so dangerous.

We settle with

the embers and specks,

the smell intoxicating,

clouding around us

with grey and black

smoke distinctly ignited,

and ablaze,

a mesmerizing

hallucination,

caught in a hypnotizing

gaze.

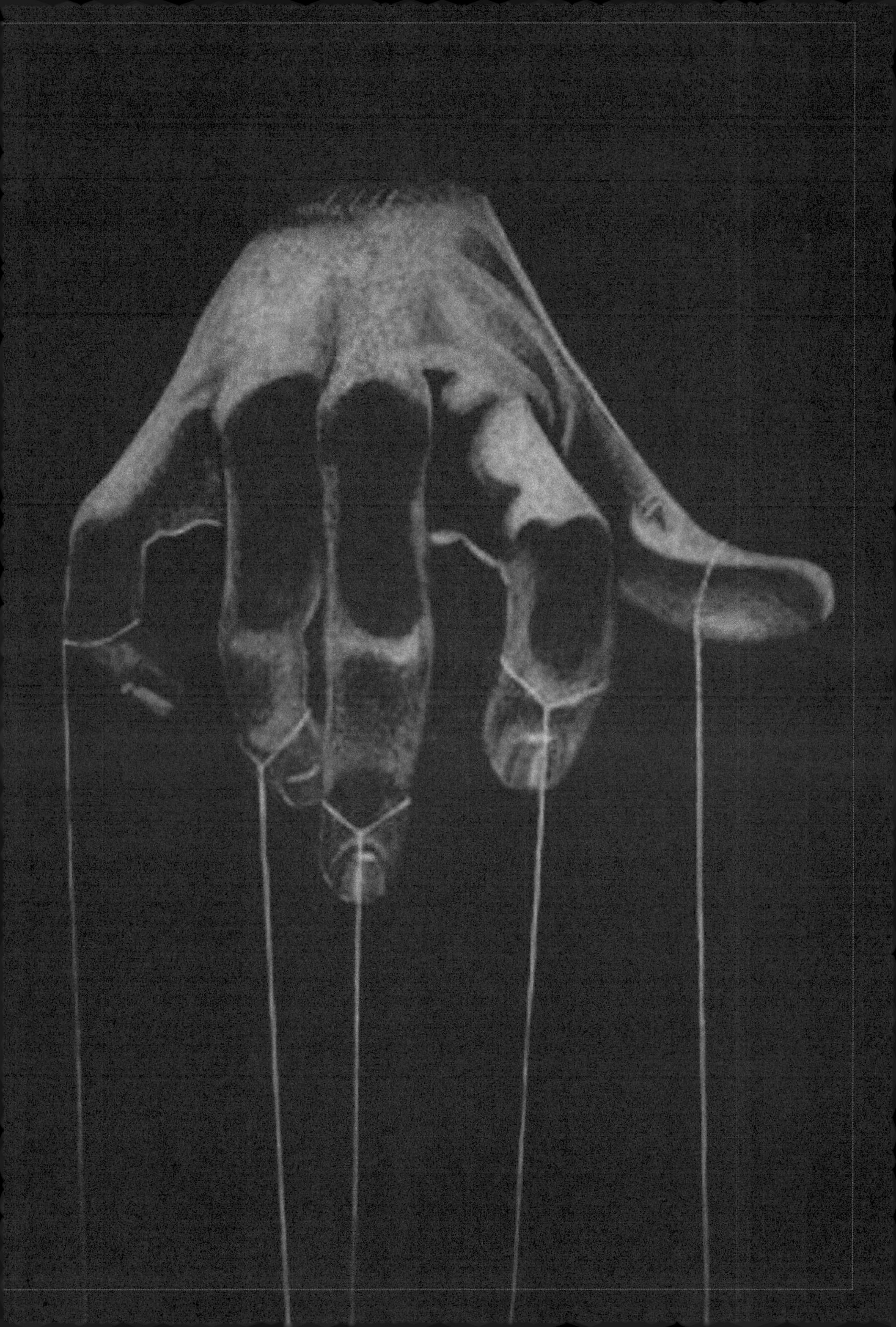

18

The Sins of Genocide

Greed, Sloth, Wrath, Envy, Lust, Gluttony, and Pride

"The Money Grows on Trees,"

They say—

A distraction,

A home invasion,

The slow and fast

Erasure

Of a people,

A history,

With articulate calculation.

It was planned—

The correlation—

A sickness,

And a weakness,

Gluttony and murder.

So obvious,

A hilarious joke,

They bask in its ambience,

To take and take,

And confiscate.

And to those who have none, or little at all,

It's a struggle:

A struggle to live,

A struggle to wake,

A struggle to stay alive—

And living just to wait.

They eat a crumb

While those live to eat.

They ride their fancy cars

While those walk in defeat.

They say,

"It's all a game.

Do you play?"

This game—a shamble,

A gamble,

A prize to be claimed.

There is a price to all this fame.

If you're very careful,

You can see the fake.

But they don't know we have matches

While they burn our homes and our names.

To all the greed,

And to all the hate,

It's a constant struggle,

A fight to keep all afloat—

Away from water,

Off the land, Off the state.

The political hunger,

While the poor are hungry—

The rich fix their faces

And play golf with their golden clubs.

Shrewd and cowardly,

They steal our keys

While the poor man struggles

To find water clean.

A struggle tired,

A struggle watched.

They put on their faces of lies

And turn off their clocks,

Because they don't respect time

And hijack, and commit crimes.

At a constant speed,

Their lust feeds

Their expensive pants pockets

While all others cry.

Under the rubble,

They sink and drown,

Under the bombs and rockets,

Wishing they could die.

Built with anger,

Defile the Earth and its soil—

The mountains of schemes.

Those clown eyes drink up blood,

Dissolving the massacre

With their spoils,

Ruins, and slaughter.

Can you see it now?

They grin with laughter.

The Power?

The destruction and violence—

They higher their bids and higher their stakes,

While the poor eat grass

And they devour their caviar and steaks.

So tell me,

In a lesson so old—

Why is this happening still?

I ask you:

In this Moral Decay,

Will the ones with all this money and power

Ever be satisfied?

Or is this the final price

We all must pay?

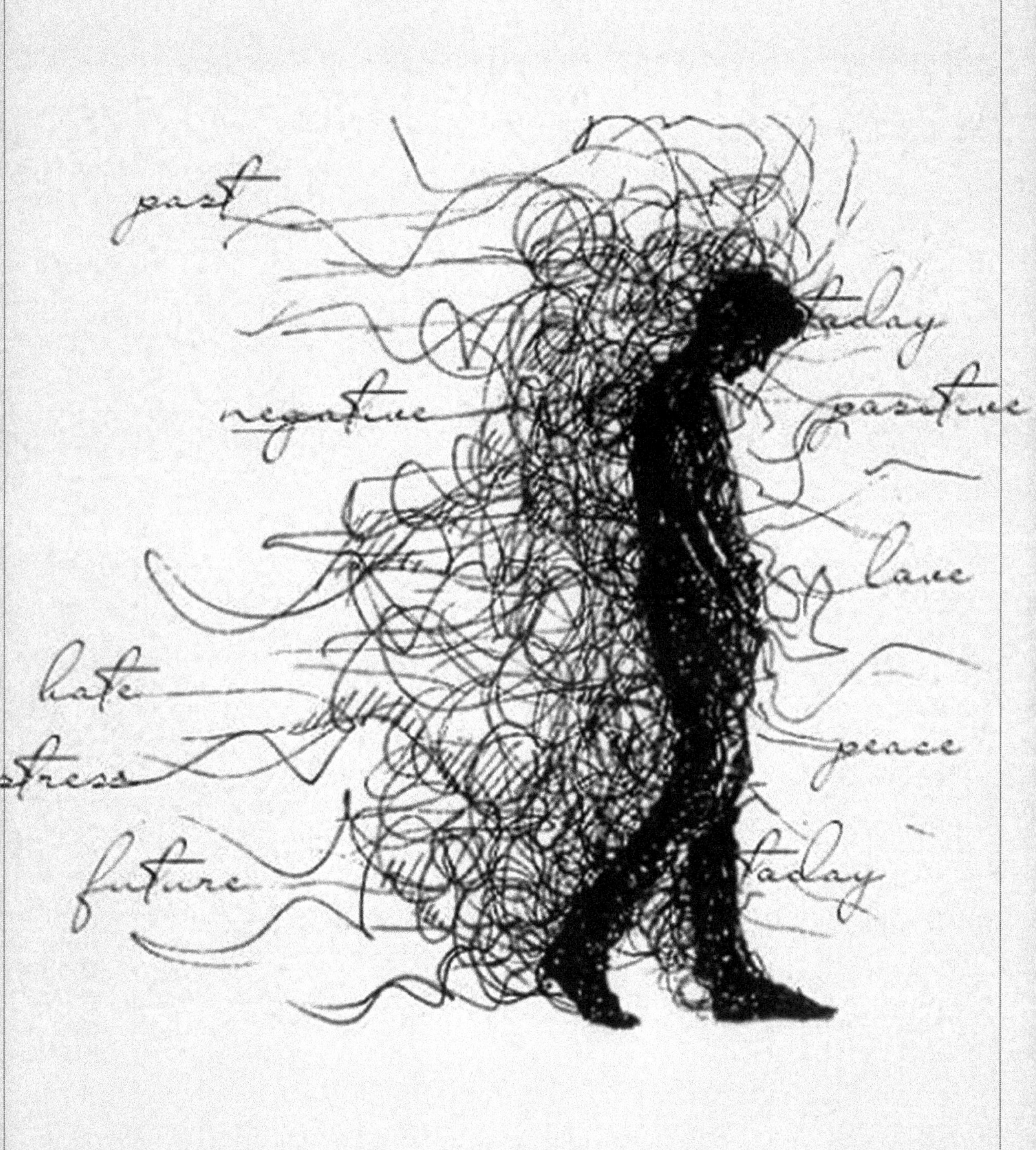
past
today
negative
positive
love
hate
peace
stress
future
today

19

The Better For You

Better not to become

attached.

Better not to become

matched.

Better not to become

a tangent, emotionless,

purposeless.

Better not to become

Like him or her.

Revel in defiance.

Have nothing else.

Better than to grovel,

pout or whine,

to complain or beg.

Apologize?

Maybe.

Better not to fall

in defeat.

Better for you, not to

get sucked in,

fucked up, trampled

over and over again.

Better for you to hide

that monster.

Better you should give:

elegance, love,

and kindness,

and more.

Better you should bury:

"the hate,"

"the anger,"

"the malice."

Better for your fate

to be unrecognizable,

unfathomable,

be uncomfortable.

Better not to become

that which is not you

ungodly, unsubmissably,

unwillingly.

Be that which can reflect

the good that you are,

and that you do.

20

The Resistance

An Ode to my Palestinian Ancestors and Palestinian Culture

She was born in a land

of olives and watermelon seeds,

Pomegranates, oranges

hummus and zataar leaves.

She thrived off the words

of her ancestors.

She strived to grow smarter

from the gardens and the farmers.

She stood taller

from her cities

and the pride of her people.

The threads of her cloth

To tell stories

In the stitches

To dress the women

and the dough

that she kneaded

into freshly baked bread

to feed the children.

The thoughts and voices

from the poetry and music

floated in the songs

With the winds

That carried and came from her heart's drive

to keep her blood and culture alive.

21

The Moon & The Flower

When the moon

fell in love with the flower,

he didn't just love her petalsa

he loved the way she

shined in his light.

He knew it was rare

to find a beauty

a flower

that bloomed and opened

up in the dark.

He knew when it does

happen,

there is nothing quite like it.

She gave all her beauty

and care to him.

The moon transitioned

every day, and then the flower

came to die.

And all of her

went back into the earth.

He was so saddened

to see her go.

He enjoyed every second

they had shared

together.

That's why the moon

disappears once a month:

to mourn his shining,

bright light his true

blossomed prize.

22

The Forgetful

In the Memory of My Loving Father

Please don't forget me

because you have.

You forgot my name,

Your eldest, your first.

In these memories

of sadness,

I take to you as a plea.

I mourn you as you

once were to me.

Your tongue, heavy.

All your words gone.

You moved with no purpose,

going backwards

when time always

continued forward....

Mad at yourself

and frustrated with us,

we try to understand

the pain.

You yell, you curse us;

your mind

an enigma, a puzzle

we cannot solve.

You slowly fade –

"My Daughter." You used to say

Shake your head

"I used to know

I used to be

I used to write

And read

I used to do so much"

Dissipate, disappearing

into the background.

No noise, just a shadow

A hollow shell

Of a person who once was.

A quiet fury,

as we anticipate

your silence that

we must bury.

23

The Time

He says, *"Do you know how to stop time?"*

"I wish I knew," she said to him.

Time stops for no man.

It's boundless to no one,

has no beginning or end.

If only we could find a way

to keep it still

to hold the day,

each hour, minute, and second,

to make it longer.

It goes against our wills,

and precisely,

it spills its ink onto paper

each person's history

and each person's future.

It binds us to memories

and moments

we change with time

grow, older.

Tokens that remind us -

it won't last.

and time accounts to no one,

has no obedience.

Like a wild child

running freely,

with absolutely

no responsibility.

To us, we question it loudly

what reliability?

Begging for it to stay,

to lengthen it

for just a little more.

But.....

For each one of us,

it decides

when to open or close its doors

and to set the sun on us,

forevermore.

24

The Unspoken Words

This is my poetry,

my language,

my everything.

I take a chance,

knowing maybe

No one will understand it.

I gather thoughts,

and these words

unfold beneath on hand,

the pen sliding smoothly

over the paper.

This is my song,

my story in my words,

layered with my life,

filled with spirited descriptions.

No need to shout or scream

No need to speak or try,

because these words cannot

pass away, fade, or die.

Staining the pages,

carrying and leading

My heavy heart, enrages it

All born from the gasping,

the grasping for air,

to find a breath.

Chances are given,

and taken away

Yet this remains:

a door kept open,

providing some strength.

A witness, proof of time,

an opinion, a soul guaranteed

by its own

sublime conscience.

And through it all,

My mind is made whole

and the book is my guaranteed essence.